This igloo book belongs to:

....

igloobooks

Published in 2013
by Igloo Books Ltd
Cottage Farm
Sywell
NN6 0BJ
www.igloobooks.com

Copyright© 2012 Igloo Books Ltd

SHE001 0613
4 6 8 10 9 7 5
ISBN 978-0-85780-570-6

Printed and manufactured in China
Illustrated by Hannah Wood

My First
Stories
for Girls

igloobooks

Contents

Sophie's Safari

"I'm going on a safari," said Princess Sophie to the queen one day. "I want to find fierce, wild animals that roar and growl!"

Sophie borrowed the king's binoculars and his water bottle.
"Right, I'm off into the jungle," she said. She kissed her
mother and set off into the palace garden.

"First, I'll explore the grasslands," said Sophie, as she
crept across the lawn. Suddenly, she saw a long, orange tail.
"It's a fierce tiger!" she cried, but it was only Fluffy, the royal cat.

Then, Sophie lay down in the long grass and peered through
her binoculars again. "Now I can see a giant tortoise,"
she said, but it was just a garden snail sliding by.

Sophie found a long, wiggly pink snake and a scary, yellow bird.
Suddenly, Sophie heard a rustling sound. It was coming closer and closer.
"What could that be?" Sophie wondered, as two pairs of giant feet appeared.

When Sophie looked up she saw her mum and dad. "We've brought you some cookies and lemonade," the king said. Sophie was very happy. Being on safari was great fun, but cookies and lemonade were better!

The Perfect Fairy Picnic

It was a bright, sunny day in Fairyland and the little fairies wanted to have fun. "Let's go to Rainbow Meadow and sit in the sun," said Buttercup. Suddenly, the Fairy Queen appeared. "Not so fast little fairies, I have some jobs for you to do," she said.

"Buttercup, I need you to find ten pretty toadstools," said the queen. The little fairies groaned. Doing jobs was boring. Buttercup sighed and fluttered off into the woodland. "I'd much rather bake some tasty treats for a picnic," she said.

13

"Tulip," said the Fairy Queen. "I need you take this basket and fill it with juicy berries." Tulip took the basket and flittered off. "I'd much rather sit in the sun in my new dress," she thought.

"Blossom, I need you to go to the lemonade stream and fill these bottles with fresh lemonade," said the Fairy Queen. Blossom flew off. "I'd much rather be drinking tasty lemonade in the sunshine," she thought.

"I have a special job for you, Petal," said the Fairy Queen.
"I need you to go to the Fairy Market and buy lots of delicious sweets."
"I'd much rather be eating the sweets," Petal grumbled as she arrived at the market.

Later, the little fairies returned with pretty toadstools, a basket
overflowing with juicy berries, bottles of lemonade and bags of the tastiest sweets.
They looked at all the delicious things, wishing that they could enjoy them.

Suddenly, the Fairy Queen appeared. "Thank you, little fairies," she said. "I know the jobs were boring, but I have a special treat for you."

"It's a surprise picnic!" said the Fairy Queen.
"You worked very hard and this is your reward."
The little fairies cheered and happily tucked into all the tasty treats.

The Princess and the Peas

Princess Poppy didn't like peas. She tried to hide them in her mashed potato, but the queen always found out. "Eat up your peas," she said, but Princess Poppy just shook her head.

Poppy hid peas under her plate. She even hid them in her crown, but the queen
always noticed. "I just don't like peas," said Princess Poppy.

21

"Our royal peas are magic," said the queen. "Come with me and I will show you."
She and the king took Princess Poppy outside to the palace vegetable patch.
The king picked a big, juicy pod and popped it open.

"If you eat these lovely fresh peas," said the king, "you'll grow up to be a queen." Poppy's eyes sparkled. She took the pea and ate it. "It's really nice," she said. After that, she never hid her peas again.

Birthday Surprise

It was the queen's birthday and Princess Amelia wanted to make her a special card. She got out her pencils, paints and brushes. She gathered her glitter, glue and a big piece of purple paper.

"I'll make a card with a picture of me on it," said Princess Amelia.
She began to draw a shape onto the card. She added flowers
around it. Then Amelia began to paint.

"I think I'll use some pink paint first," said Princess Amelia.
By accident, she knocked over the paint pot and it spilled all over her picture.

"Oh, no!" cried Princess Amelia. "Now Mum's card is ruined."
Just then, Kitty jumped up to see what was going on. Her tail swished across
the glue and blue glittery stars, sending sparkles everywhere.

"I'd better finish this in the palace garden," said Princess Amelia.
"It's getting rather messy." She sat on the bench and looked at
the picture. "I suppose it isn't too bad," she thought.

A sudden gust of wind picked up the card and blew it straight into the rose bush.
Just as Amelia was pulling it out, she heard the queen calling.

29

Amelia grabbed her card and ran inside. "Happy birthday, Mum!"
cried Princess Amelia, giving her mother a big cuddle.
"I've made you a card, but it went a bit wrong," she added, sadly.

The queen looked at the card and smiled, happily.

"That's the best birthday card ever," she said, giving Amelia a big smile.

"It's beautiful because it's a picture of you!"

Honeybell's Holiday

It was the last day of the holiday for Honeybell and her friends. They were having fun at the Fairytale Fair. "I'm going on the bouncy castle," said Silverwing. "Whee!" said Honeybell, on the rollercoaster. "I'll take your photograph," said Cherrybud.

Next, Honeybell whirled around on the carousel. Then she jumped
and jiggled on the bouncy castle. She even won a wand for bouncing
the highest. "I wish my holiday would never end," she giggled.

When the fairies visited the sparkly Blue Lagoon, Honeybell pretended to be a mermaid. She splashed her friend Cherrybud, then swam away. Silverwing thought it was so funny that she took lots of photos.

When it was time to go back to the Fairy Forest,
Honeybell felt very sad. She had done so many amazing
things on her holiday, how would she remember them all?

"Don't worry, Honeybell," said Cherrybud, when they got back to the forest.

"I've just had a wonderful idea that will cheer you up."

She took out a glue stick and a big book with blank pages.

"It's a scrapbook," explained Silverwing. "We'll stick in all the photos, tickets and pictures from our holiday to make a book of special memories." Honeybell smiled. "Now I'll never forget our happy holiday," she said.

The Busy Princess

It was breakfast time at the pink palace. Princess Ruby was in a very bad mood. "Everyone's busy except me," she moaned, dropping her silver spoon onto the table and nearly knocking over her porridge.

"It's boring being a princess," said Ruby. "I want do interesting
things like everyone else." She thought for a moment.
"I know! I'll bake a cake," said Ruby as she ran excitedly to the kitchen.

Cook got the ingredients ready, but Princess Ruby got so much flour everywhere that it made everyone sneeze. Then, she slopped cake mixture all down her lovely dress. "This is far too messy," said Ruby.

Princess Ruby thought that gardening would be fun.

"I'll water the flowers," she said, turning on the hosepipe.

It wiggled wildly and the water burst out. "Oh, no!" cried Ruby. "I'm all wet."

Next, Ruby decided she would have a go at grooming her pony, Moonshine. The comb got stuck in his mane and he neighed, stamping his feet. "Oh, no!" she cried. "This is too scary."

Ruby wandered over to the dressmaker, who was carefully sewing
buttons onto Ruby's favourite dress. "Let me have a go," said Ruby,
grabbing a needle. "Ouch!" she cried, as she pricked her finger.

43

"Maybe the maid's job will be easy," said Ruby.
She polished the mirrors and swept the floors,
but it was very hard work. "This is far too tiring," she grumbled.

Ruby got into her comfy royal bed. She looked around at her beautiful, clean dresses and her pretty things. "I think being a Princess isn't so bad after all," she said, smiling happily. After her busy day, Princess Ruby never complained again.

Fairy Cakes

Twinkle and Sparkle had just been given their wands. "Let's magic up some delicious treats to celebrate," suggested Twinkle. Whoosh! went her wand, but instead of a fairy cake, a mouldy apple appeared.

"Yuck!" cried Sparkle. "That doesn't look very tasty. Let me try." She swished her wand and a pile of burnt toast appeared. The fairies were really disappointed. "If we can't do magic, then we aren't proper fairies," they said, sadly.

"Maybe because we're little, our magic isn't strong enough. I think we should try together," said Sparkle. The two fairies both waved their wands and wished as hard as they could.

48

The mouldy apple turned into a bunch of juicy fruit.
The toast became a stack of tasty sandwiches. "We did it!"
they laughed. "We really are proper fairies after all."

Princess Mona

Princess Mona wasn't in a very good mood. First, she moaned about her soggy cereal. "There's too much milk," grumbled Mona. Then, she complained about her dress. "There are too many frills," she frowned.

After breakfast, her mother tried to brush Mona's curly hair.

"OUCH!" howled Mona, as the queen tugged at a tangle.

"Go and play in the garden," said the queen. "Maybe that will cheer you up."

Mona stomped outside and sat on the see-saw. "I'm bored," she moaned. Picking up her skipping rope, Mona started to skip. "One, two, three, WHOOPS!" she said as she tripped on the rope and fell onto the grass.

Feeling crosser than ever, Mona bounced her ball against the wall.

Suddenly, it bounced over the top and disappeared.

"I wish I had someone to play with," muttered Mona.

Just then, a girl peeped over the wall and waved the ball at Mona.
"My name's Hannah and I've just moved in next door," she said.
"I found your ball, do you want to play?"

The two girls had a lovely time together. They played catch,
went up and down on the see-saw and even had a skipping race.
"Now I've got a friend," said Mona, "I don't need to moan anymore!"

55

The Princess Twins

It was a sunny day and Princess Lucy was having a tea party in the palace garden. Suddenly, her sister, Princess Polly, whizzed by on her bike, right over the picnic rug.

"Princesses shouldn't ride bikes!" cried Lucy.
"You've squashed my cupcakes and upset Kitty."
"Whoops, sorry," said Princess Polly, as she rode off.

When Lucy was practicing ballet, Polly burst in kicking her ball.

The ball flew through the air and Lucy had to duck.

"Why can't you behave like a proper princess?" she wailed.

That afternoon, Lucy was playing her violin when there was a loud
banging and clattering. Polly was playing her drums. "You're so annoying!"
shouted Lucy, angrily. "Why can't you just be a proper princess?"

Later, Lucy was painting in the garden when she
heard a loud meowing from the trees. It was Kitty and she was stuck.
"Help, help!" cried Lucy but no one came.

Suddenly, Polly came bouncing over on her pogo stick.

"I'll get Kitty," she said and she quickly climbed the tree.

"Thank you!" cried Lucy. "I'm really glad you're not a proper princess after all!"

The Pink Bike

It was Princess Emma's birthday and the king had given her a new, pink bike. She climbed onto it and cried, "I'm ready to ride!"

"Wait," called the king. "I've got something else for you."

Princess Emma was too excited to wait and wobbled off round the palace garden.

"Look, I'm riding my bike!" She shouted, swerving round the dog.

She bounced over the hosepipe and knocked down a row of flowerpots.

Princess Emma tried to steer around the sandpit and the bird table but the bike would not stop wobbling. She whizzed through the cook's special vegetable patch, squashing the cabbages.

"Oh no!" cried Princess Emma as she bumped and bounced across the lawn.

The pink bike flattened the queen's flowers, then toppled over.

Emma fell off and landed in a pile of leaves.

"I don't like riding my new bike," cried Princess Emma.
"At least you had a soft landing," said the king, coming out of
the shed with two little wheels. He fixed them to her bike.

"These will help your balance," the king promised.
Princess Emma wasn't sure, but she climbed back onto the bike and tried again.
To her amazement, it stopped wobbling. "Now I really can ride my bike," she said.

The Clumsy Fairy

The fairies were flying to the summer ball. They had spent ages getting ready. "Hurry up," said Lillybelle, "We'll be late." Cherryblossom didn't look where she was going. Suddenly she went THWACK! into a tree.

Cherryblossom fell with a splosh, into a puddle. "Oh, no," she said.
"My dress is torn and I'm all muddy and wet. I can't go to the ball like this."
"Don't worry," replied her friends, "We'll help you."

"Wait here," they told Cherryblossom and each fairy flew off in a different direction. "My dress is ruined," said Cherryblossom. "I'm late for the ball and now my friends have left me!"

After a while, Silverwing appeared. She smiled and held out a beautiful pink dress. "Thank you," replied Cherryblossom, "but my hat is still wet and my shoes are dirty."

Lilybelle and Starshine suddenly appeared.

They handed Cherryblossom a beautiful pair of shoes and a pretty hat.

"You're the best friends ever!" cried Cherryblossom. "Now I can go to the ball!"

Cherryblossom put on the lovely dress, the shiny shoes and pretty hat.
Everyone had a wonderful time at the summer ball and after that,
Cherryblossom made sure she always looked where she was flying!

Willow the Weather Fairy

"I want the weather to be perfect for my party today," said the Fairy Queen.
Willow was worried that if she couldn't make it sunny, the queen would be cross.

"I've only just learned weather magic,
but I'll do my best," said Willow, rushing outside to practise.
"Wave my wand to the right, make the sun shine bright," she said.

At once, the clouds disappeared and the the sun shone brightly.
In fact, it was very warm. "Phew! It's too hot now," gasped Willow
as she sat down in the shade under a toadstool.

Fanning herself with a leaf, Willow cast another spell.
"Tap my wand on my knees, make a cool refreshing breeze!" she said.
Suddenly, a big gust of wind swept through the palace garden.

The wind was so strong that it blew away all the party decorations. "What have I done?" cried Willow. Quickly, she waved her wand and said, "Make the wind go away and cool us down another way!"

Straight away the wind stopped and a gentle rain
started pitter-pattering down. "Oh, no," said Willow.
"Not rain! Now the party really will be ruined."

79

With a magical flash, the Fairy Queen appeared.
"Thank you for the perfect party weather, Willow," she smiled.
"Raindrops make everything sparkle and a rainbow is a wonderful decoration."

Willow sighed with relief. The sun shone gently as she joined in the fun. The rainbow stayed, filling the sky with its glowing colours. It really was the perfect party day.

Rosie's Race

It was the day of the Royal Summer Sports day.

"I bet I can beat you!" said Prince John to his sister, Princess Rosie.

When the whistle blew, he started running. But Princess Rosie had a secret.

Rosie could run really fast. She raced off ahead of her brother.
Prince John was so amazed that he stumbled and tripped over.

Rosie stopped and ran back to her brother.
"Are you all right?" she asked, as she helped him up.
John nodded. "I'm fine but I'll never win the race now," he said.

"We can finish it together," said Rosie. Holding hands,
they ran all the way to the finishing line. Everyone cheered.
"Thank you, Rosie," said Prince John. "Next time, I'll remember to be as kind as you!"

The Fairy Friends

It was the day of the fairy ball and everyone in Fairyland was excited.
Dewdrop and Mayflower raced to Miss Sunshine's
dress shop to buy pretty new party dresses.

The fairies tried on lots of dresses until they found the perfect outfits.

Picking up a pretty pink wand, Mayflower said. "This will look lovely with my dress."

"That's the wand I want," said Dewdrop.

"Be careful!" said Miss Sunshine, but the fairies weren't listening. Mayflower snatched the wand from Dewdrop. "I saw it first, it's mine," she said. "No, it's mine!" cried Dewdrop, grabbing the wand.

The two fairies pulled and tugged. Suddenly, the wand snapped in half.
Dewdrop and Mayflower fell backwards with a crash. "You've broken my prize wand
and ruined my shop!" cried Miss Sunshine. "Please leave."

Outside, the fairies slumped on a toadstool. They had broken the special wand and they didn't have new dresses. "It's not nice when we fight," said Dewdrop. Mayflower agreed and they went inside to apologize to Miss Sunshine.

Miss Sunshine was very kind. She wrapped up their dresses and even found them two matching wands. The fairies both promised that from now on, they would never, ever fallout again.

The Dance Class

The music started at Princess Daisy's first royal ballet class.
All around, the other princesses whirled and twirled, gracefully.
Daisy tried her best to follow them, but her feet got in a muddle.

THUMP! Daisy fell to the floor. She felt really silly. "I can't do it," she said. "Don't worry," said a friendly voice. It was Princess Rose. "It's always hard to begin with. Just keep practicing and you'll soon get better."

Daisy practiced really hard. A few weeks later,
she was standing on one leg, pointing her toes and holding her
arms up in the air. It was a bit wobbly, but she did it!

At the next class, Daisy whirled and twirled with the other dancers.
Then she heard a thump and someone said, "Ouch!"
It was the new girl, Princess Lily. Daisy helped her up.

"I fell over in my first lesson, too," said Daisy. "Don't worry, you just need practice!" She took Lily's hand and before long, they were whirling around having a wonderful time.